*In loving memory of
my aunt 'Josey', Jo Claire Phillips;
and my aunts Vera and Arlene;*

*and in loving honor of my aunts
Helen, Betty, and Christine.*

Thanks for loving me my whole life!

Love, Kathy

Text © 2005 by Kathleen Long Bostrom

Illustrated by Frank Ordaz

Design: The DesignWorks Group,
www.thedesignworksgroup.com

Published in 2005 by
Broadman & Holman Publishers,
Nashville, Tennessee

DEWEY: CE
SUBHD: CHRISTMAS—FICTION \ GIVING—FICTION

10-Digit ISBN: 0-8054-3020-2
13-Digit ISBN: 978-0-8054-3020-2

1 2 3 4 5   09 08 07 06 05

Josie's Gift

KATHLEEN LONG BOSTROM

Illustrated by FRANK ORDAZ

BROADMAN & HOLMAN PUBLISHERS

Nashville, Tennessee

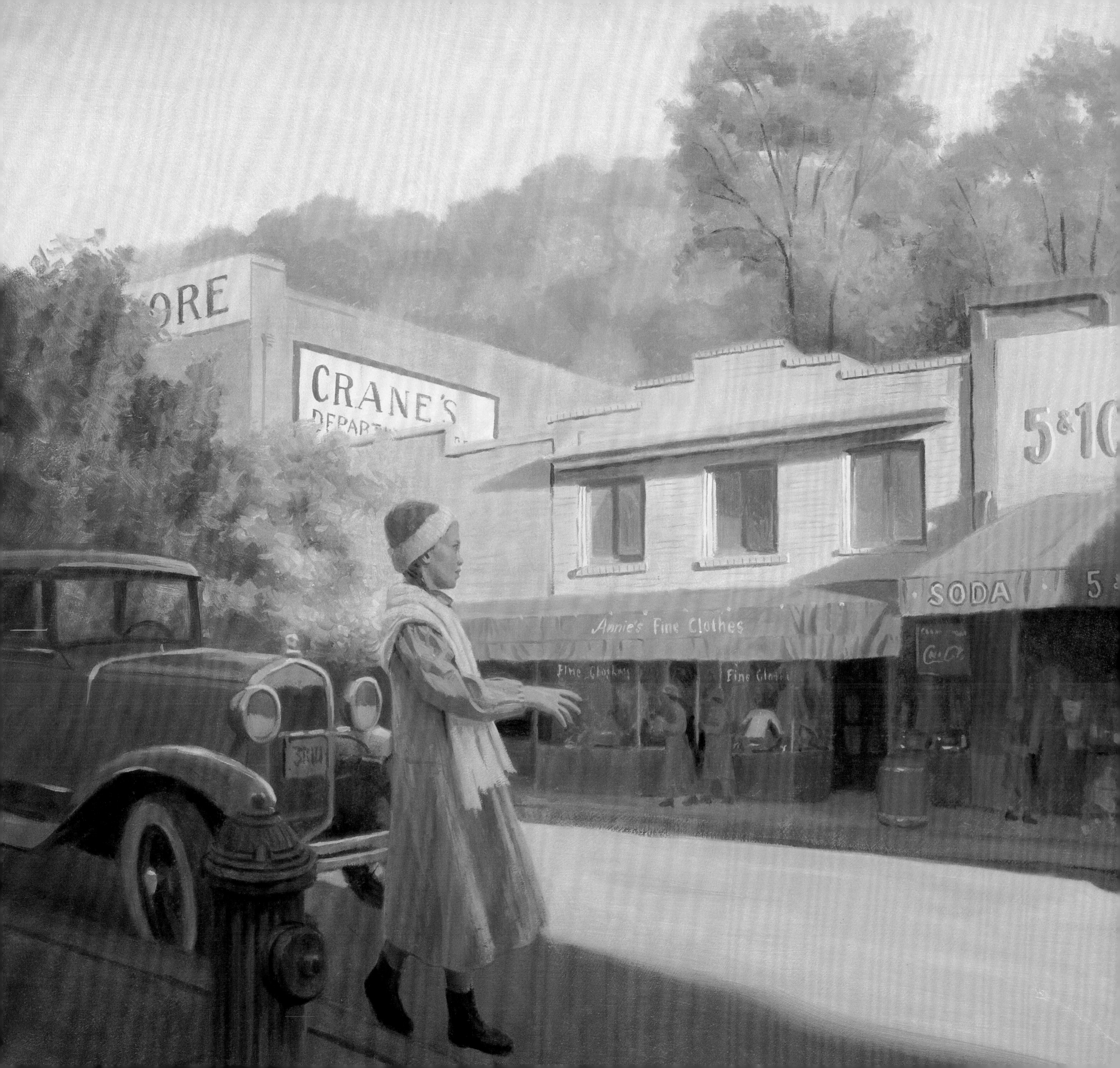
ORE
CRANE'S
SODA
Annie's Fine Clothes

JOSIE KNEW EXACTLY what she wanted for Christmas that year, the first Christmas after Papa died. She knew as deep down sure as a person could get that this was the one gift she absolutely had to have.

Josie would never forget the day she first saw the blue sweater. The crisp, October air made Josie's cheeks turn pink as she rode into town with Mama and her little brother Bobby Joe on their weekly shopping trip. Garden patches spilled over with plump, orange pumpkins. Josie took deep breaths and could almost smell the spicy pies she and Mama would be baking soon with some of those pumpkins.

While Mama did her shopping at the *Five and Dime,* Josie wandered next door to check out the window display of her favorite clothing store. Usually, she was satisfied with just looking at the elegant clothes, some with sequins that sparkled like rubies and emeralds. She knew her family would never be able to afford such luxuries.

Still, Josie dreamed about wearing the fancy dresses with purses to match. She tilted her head as if she were wearing a hat with silk flowers stitched to its sweeping brim. She closed her eyes and pretended to dance in the spike-heeled shoes that came in every color of the rainbow.

But on that fall day when Josie peeked in the window of the store, there it was: a sweater, blue as the blue of the summer sky, blue as Josie's eyes, the prettiest blue she'd ever seen in all her life.

Why, it's just so beautiful! she sighed, staring at the blue sweater draped gracefully against sparkling white tissue paper. She counted twelve shimmering, pearl-white buttons down the front of the sweater, and reached her hand to the window as if she could feel the softness of the fine knit through the glass.

Every week after that, when Mama, Josie, and Bobby Joe made their trip to town, Josie stopped in front of the shop window so she could gaze at the blue sweater.

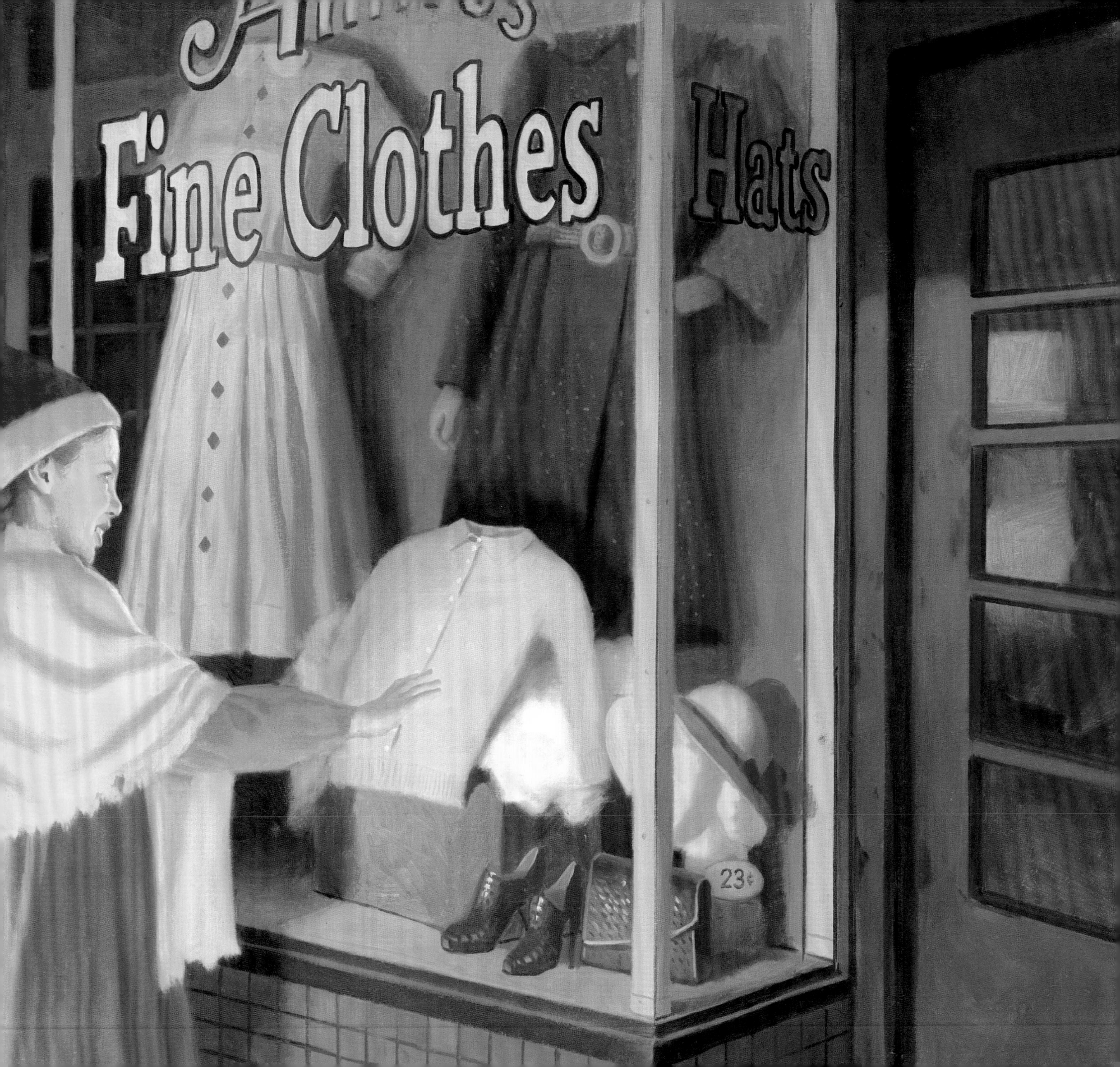
Fine Clothes
Hats
23¢

"Mama," Josie announced to her mother in the kitchen one day, "I know what I want for Christmas."

Josie's mother pushed her wooden rolling pin back and forth across a mound of pie dough with her sleeves rolled up. Without missing a beat, she said to Josie, "And what would that be, Josie-girl?"

Josie winced at the nickname her Papa had pinned on her back when she was younger than Bobby Joe was now. It was Papa's special name for her. "Josie-girl," Papa would say as she tagged along on his chores, "hand me that milk bucket," or "Josie-girl, now you be careful near those hogs or you'll be swimming in their supper." It just didn't sound the same, coming from Mama.

"Mama, you know that blue sweater in the dress shop window? Why, it's the prettiest thing I've ever seen! It has twelve pearl-white buttons—twelve! Mama, if I can have that sweater for Christmas, I promise I'll never ask for anything again!"

Mama stopped her rolling. "Now, Josie-girl, don't you go making promises you can't keep."

"But Mama, I mean it. This sweater is the most beautiful thing I've ever seen, and I don't ask for much, and I never wanted anything more in my life. Mama, please!"

Mama dusted the flour from her hands and brushed a loose strand of hair from her eyes. "I know it's a lovely sweater, Josie," she sighed, "but we can't afford things like that. You know there's a Depression going on. With Papa gone, why, it's all I can do to keep this farm going and everyone fed." Mama pushed the rolling pin through the dough, a little harder than before. "I'm sorry, Josie-girl." Even though Josie knew her mother truly was sorry, she ran from the room without another word.

Tucked into bed that night, Josie thought about the Christmases they'd had when Papa was alive. On Christmas Eve, they would all go to church. Everyone got a small, unlit candle when they came in the door. At the end of the service the pastor lit a tall white candle called the Christ candle. One-by-one, each person in the church lit their candle from the Christ candle until the whole church glowed. They all sang *Silent Night* and *Joy to the World* and Josie's spirit swelled with such happiness that she felt full to the brim.

Back home, Papa always lit a fire while Mama made steaming mugs of hot chocolate and buttered bread with brown sugar and cinnamon, a special treat. Then Papa took a carved, wooden box from the cedar chest and set it carefully on the floor in front of the fireplace while the two children sat waiting. Bobby Joe nearly jumped out of his skin with excitement.

Papa lifted the lid on the box, then reached inside. Tenderly, he lifted the little figures wrapped in soft scraps of cloth.

Every year, Papa carved a wooden figure for the nativity he had started on Josie's first Christmas. First, he carved Mary, the next year Joseph, and when Josie turned three, a tiny wooden manger and a baby appeared in the nativity on Christmas morning. The year Josie was four and Bobby Joe was born, Papa added a shepherd. Soon, the nativity included Mary and Joseph, the baby, one shepherd, two sheep, a wise man, and a cow. It became a guessing game, wondering what figure Papa would carve next.

On Christmas Eve, as the children set out the wooden pieces on the slate hearth by the fireplace, Papa and Josie had fun remembering the order in which the pieces had been carved.

"Mary was the first," Papa said.

"Then came Joseph," said Josie.

"Next came the baby Jesus."

"And then the shepherd and the sheep!"

"Not fair, Josie-girl!" Papa laughed. "You got to count two!"

"You count the next two," Josie smiled.

"OK," said Papa. "The wise man and the cow."

Bobby Joe looked puzzled. "Did the wise man ride on a cow?"

Papa whisked Bobby Joe into his arms and whirled him around, tickling the little boy's face with his rough beard. "Yes, that's it, Bobby Joe!" Papa's hearty laugh filled the room. "The wise man rode to Bethlehem on a cow!" That year, Papa added a camel to the growing crowd gathered around the baby Jesus.

After all the figures were in place, Papa settled into his big chair near the fire. Bobby Joe snuggled under one of Papa's big, strong arms while Josie tucked herself under the other. Mama rocked next to them in the chair Papa had made for her when Josie was born.

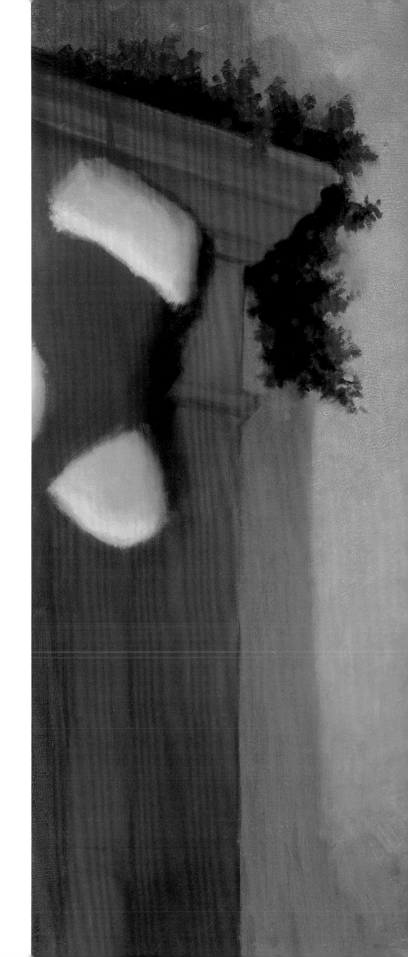

Papa had a saying. "Remember," he said every year, "Christmas is not about what we want. It's about what we have." Then he'd kiss both children on the forehead. They'd sit by the fire until Josie and Bobby Joe fell asleep, then Papa carried them to bed.

But that spring Papa died of the fever, and Josie knew that nothing would ever be the same.

Summer passed, and then fall, and winter came. Soon, it would be Christmas. Christmas without Papa. Josie tried to think about the blue sweater and not about Papa because she couldn't bear the thought of Christmas without him.

On Christmas Eve, Mama, Josie, and Bobby Joe went to church. They lit their candles from the Christ candle and sang *Silent Night* and *Joy to the World*, although there was little joy in Josie's world. She felt as deep down empty as a person could get.

Back home, Josie lit the fire while Mama made steaming mugs of hot chocolate and buttered bread with brown sugar and cinnamon. Josie and Bobby Joe sat by the fireplace and watched as Mama took the carved, wooden box from the cedar chest and set it on the slate hearth in front of them.

Mama lifted the lid on the box, then reached inside. One-by-one, she handed Josie and Bobby Joe the little figures wrapped in soft scraps of cloth. Mary, Joseph, the baby Jesus and the manger, one shepherd, two sheep, a wise man, a cow, and a camel. Nine figures, as there always, only would be.

"Will there be a new figure in the nativity tomorrow?" Bobby Joe asked hopefully.

"Of course not!" Josie said sharply. She saw the stricken look on her little brother's face, and quickly wrapped her arms around him.

"No, Bobby Joe," she said gently. "There won't be any new figures in the nativity tomorrow. There will never again be a new one."

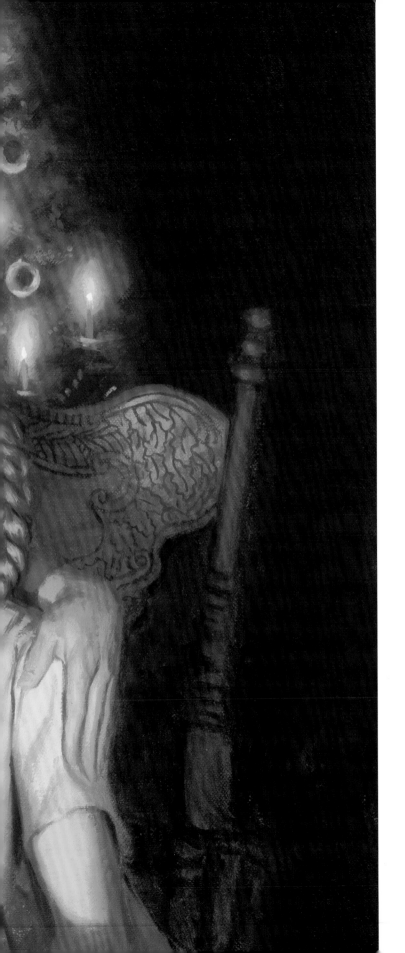

Mama sat down in Papa's chair by the fire, and Bobby Joe crawled into her lap. Josie sat in Mama's rocker. "Remember," Mama said, "Christmas is not about what we want. It's about what we have." Bobby Joe nodded sleepily, and snuggled closer to Mama. Josie sat very still.

This was the Christmas that Josie wanted more than what she had. She wanted to have Papa back again. She wanted everything to be like it used to be, and she wanted the blue sweater. Maybe the sweater would help fill the emptiness Josie felt inside.

Long after Mama and Bobby Joe fell asleep, Josie lay in bed, wide awake, fighting back the tears. "What's the point of Christmas?" she whispered to the darkness. "It's not about what we want. It's not about what we have. It's all about what's missing. That's what Christmas is."

She climbed out of bed, wrapped herself in an old, worn shawl, and tiptoed down the stairs. A few embers glowed in the fireplace and she took the metal poker and jabbed at the logs, sending sparks swirling up the chimney like winter fireflies.

Then Josie saw the box under the Christmas tree in the corner by the rocking chair. Her heart tightened and she ran over to the tree and picked up the box. She read the name on the handmade paper tag—Josie.

"Please," she whispered. "Please let this be the blue sweater." She pulled the ribbon off the box and threw the lid aside.

Carefully, Josie folded back the sparkling white tissue paper. "Oh!" she sighed as she lifted the blue sweater and held it to her cheek. Not even a cloud could feel that soft.

She dropped her old shawl to the floor, and slipped her arms through the sleeves of the sweater. One-by-one, Josie buttoned the twelve, shimmering pearl-white buttons.

She twirled around the room, then stopped to gaze at herself in the mirror. The blue matched her eyes, just as she knew it would. The sweater was perfect, everything she expected it to be.

But the emptiness remained.

Josie turned away from the mirror, and slowly walked back to the fireplace. She picked up her boots, jammed them on her bare feet and slipped out the backdoor into the freezing cold night. The vast darkness echoed the way she felt deep down inside. "God, are You there? Can You hear me?" Josie whispered into the night, but nobody answered. She wondered if Papa could see her from heaven.

Josie headed down the sloping hill to the barn. Josie had always loved the animals on the farm. She'd spent many hours in the barn, running her fingers through the woolly curls of the sheep, helping Papa milk the cows, brushing down the horses after a hard day in the fields. The animals comforted her.

Josie pushed open the barn door. She patted the two cows on their velvety brown foreheads, and scratched behind the horse's ears. She knelt down by the sheep, which were her favorites. She closed her eyes, and put her arms around the smelly, woolly neck of the smallest one.

Suddenly, Josie felt the hairs prickle on her neck. Something told her that she and the animals weren't alone in the barn.

Josie opened her eyes and stared over the back of the sheep into a dark corner of the barn. Her breath caught in her throat. Two figures crouched in the straw. One of them held a small bundle.

"Who are you? What do you want?" Josie's voice quivered as she started to back away.

The man stepped out of the shadows. "Please," he said. "We don't aim to harm you. We're heading east. My wife— my baby—they're awful cold. We're just needing a warm place to stay for the night."

Josie stared in amazement. She knew that many people had lost their homes because of the Depression. She had never thought about how it must feel to be without a home, especially on a cold December night.

"Come with me," Josie said. "You can't stay out here in the barn. It's too cold. We have room in our house. You can sleep inside by the fire. Mama won't mind."

"No," the man said. "We're fine right here. We'll stay the night and then be on our way."

The pride in the man's voice kept Josie from asking again.

The man's wife rocked back and forth in the straw, singing softly to her baby, wrapped in a ragged blanket. The baby's tiny cries made Josie think of the newborn sheep she'd helped Papa birth every spring. The woman shivered, just a bit, but Josie saw.

Carefully, Josie slowly unbuttoned the twelve, pearl-white buttons of her new blue sweater. She slipped her arms from the sleeves, held it against her cheek one last time, then reached over and tucked the sweater around the baby nestled in the mother's arms.

"Merry Christmas," Josie said.

"We can't accept no gift," the man said. "We got nothin' to give in return."

"I don't want anything," Josie said. "Besides, Christmas is not about what we want. It's about what we have. That's what my Papa always told me."

The man bowed his head in a simple gesture of thanks. The woman tucked the sweater around the now sleeping baby and brought the soft bundle to her cheek.

Josie left the barn. Halfway up the little hill to her house, she stopped and looked back. Then she tilted her head and stared up into the night. The sky no longer seemed empty.

"Thank You, God," she said softly. She didn't even notice the cold.

Once inside, Josie stood beside the fireplace, and touched each of the figures from Papa's nativity.

Mary, Joseph, the baby Jesus in a manger, one shepherd, two sheep, a wise man, a cow, and a camel.

Josie picked up the tiny, wooden baby, still wrapped in a soft scrap of cloth. She touched the figure to her cheek. She closed her eyes and smelled the sweet wood, remembering the joy she felt every year as she, Papa, Mama, and Bobby Joe gathered around the nativity and tried to guess who would be next to join the growing crowd around the baby Jesus.

Josie's heart nearly skipped a beat. She was wrong when she'd told Bobby Joe that there would never be anyone else in that nativity. She knew who would be next to kneel before the Christ child.

"It's my turn," she whispered, as she placed the tiny wooden baby back in the manger. She knelt and bowed her head in a simple prayer.

"Dear God," she prayed, "thank You for Jesus. Thank You for Christmas. I nearly missed it, but that will never happen again . . . I promise. Amen."

Slowly, Josie stood up. She wrapped herself in her old shawl and curled up in Papa's chair by the fire. She could hardly wait for Mama and Bobby Joe to come down the stairs on Christmas morning.

She felt full to the brim.

For Christmas, she knew, wasn't about what she wanted. It was about what she had, deep down in her soul that only God could give.